虎
纪
妮

NINI

François Thisdale

Tundra Books

Published in English in Canada by Tundra Books,
75 Sherbourne Street, Toronto, Ontario M5A 2P9

Published in English in the United States by Tundra Books of Northern New York,
P.O. Box 1030, Plattsburgh, New York 12901

Originally published in French in 2009 by Les Éditions Hurtubise

LIBRARY OF CONGRESS CONTROL NUMBER: 2010942902

Library and Archives Canada Cataloguing in Publication

Thisdale, François, 1964-
Nini / François Thisdale.

Originally published in French under the same title.
ISBN 978-1-77049-270-7

I. Title.

PS8639.H546N5513 2011   jC843.'6   C2011-900245-0

We acknowledge the financial support of the Government of Canada through the Book Publishing Industry Development Program (BPIDP) and that of the Government of Ontario through the Ontario Media Development Corporation's Ontario Book Initiative. We further acknowledge the support of the Canada Council for the Arts and the Ontario Arts Council for our publishing program.

 ONTARIO ARTS COUNCIL
CONSEIL DES ARTS DE L'ONTARIO

Printed and bound in China

1 2 3 4 5 6   16 15 14 13 12 11

To Nini, my little flower from Shanxi

The baby heard a voice. It promised many mysterious things.
It spoke of rice paddies and lotus flowers, blowing in the evening breeze.

The voice described a little house
with a pointed roof and a very long river
and a sun and a moon that took turns
hanging over that little house.

The voice told her of bamboo boats and bicycles
that rolled past golden fields and jagged mountains.

Sometimes, the voice spoke of things that made it sound sad.
It would falter, then stop.
In the quiet, the baby could hear bare feet on the beaten earth below her,
and farther away, a shrill cry, welcoming the sun.

For the infant, there was nothing to mark the passage of time except the voice. Warm and safe, she listened carefully to all it said.

The time came when the baby needed to see all those wondrous things for herself.
And so, she was born.
The first face she saw was the sweet face that belonged to the voice.
The first hands she felt were the soft hands of love.

党纪妮  木 况报告

党纪妮、女、2002年8月15日出生。2002年8月15日，大同市公安局……分局……万圣商场门口发现该女婴、……弃婴后，于2002年8月……院庇局取名为……

高62厘米，坐高……头围……厘米，胸长9厘米，……

党纪妮从出生到现在已有6个月，在保育员的精心照料下，……一日睡眠11个小时左右，每日7:00起床，……12:00午睡，晚上20:00就寝。睡眠安稳，入睡时爱吮吸手指，夜间醒后，帮她换好尿布，喝点开水或奶粉，然后抚摸……就能继续入睡。

……妮食欲较好，饮食以牛奶为主，日饮食6次，就餐时间为3:00、7:00、11:00、15:00、19:00、23:00，每次饮食……开水，消化良好，每日大便1—2次，

But the next day, when the infant opened her eyes,
the face and the loving hands were gone.
The only trace of the voice that had been with her for nine months
was its echo in her memory.

党纪妮，女，2001年×月×日出生。2002年8月15日，大
同市公安局稽查侦查民警在大同市东关万多商场门口发现该女婴。
经多方查找，未找到其亲生父母、确认为弃婴后，于2002年8月
15日送入大同市社会福利院监护抚养。我院按其入院先后取名为
党纪妮。该女婴据多日观察，身体健康、无任何疾病。

　　经最近体检、党纪妮体质发育情况良好。现体重6公斤，身
高62厘米，坐高39厘米，胸围41厘米、头围41厘米，脚长9
厘米、现仍未长牙。

Instead of a little house with a pointed roof, the baby lay in a large building with many rooms and many more little beds. Friendly hands lifted her to feed her and keep her clean, but they were not the soft hands that had first held her.

Many voices wailed around her, some frail, some frightened, some angry, some hopeful. Then, another wail, louder than the rest, chimed in. The baby had joined the chorus of crying orphans, each one missing a special voice and the promises it had made.

Even in their company, the tiny girl felt very much alone.

On the other side of the world, a woman rubbed her womb, encouraging new life to begin. The baby she hoped for would blossom like a flower, carefully tended by her and him. It would have all the love these two people shared to make it strong, just like seedlings have rain to warm them and nourish their roots.

But the baby did not come.

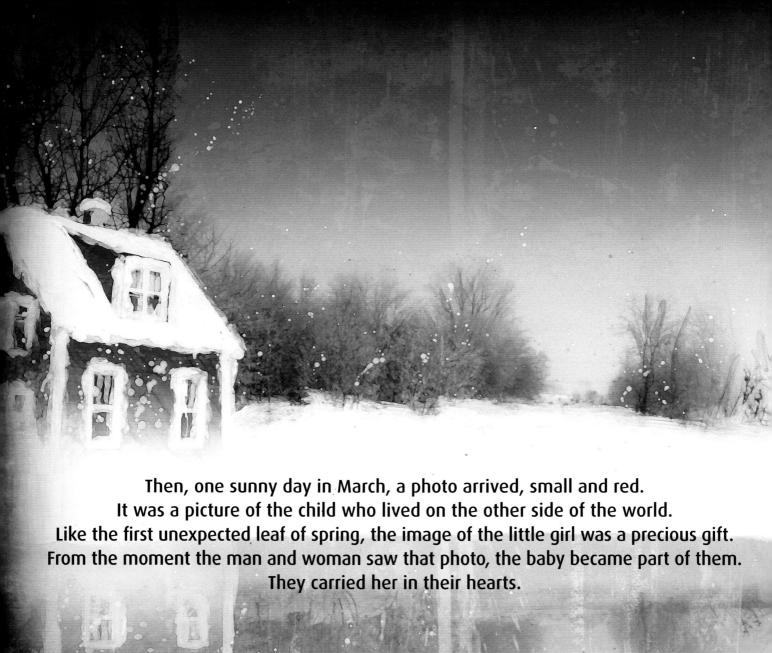

Then, one sunny day in March, a photo arrived, small and red.
It was a picture of the child who lived on the other side of the world.
Like the first unexpected leaf of spring, the image of the little girl was a precious gift.
From the moment the man and woman saw that photo, the baby became part of them.
They carried her in their hearts.

The people at the orphanage told the child that she was very lucky.
She was going on a long journey to a land of golden fields and mountains
and rivers and bicycles and boats. There would be a house with a pointed roof,
with a sun and a moon that took turns hanging over it.

A man and a woman lived there.
They had been waiting, waiting, waiting . . . for her.

Indeed, the journey was long.

Friendly hands held the little girl as they followed the winding river that flowed past mountains and away from rice paddies until it came to a large city. There, everything was different. It seemed to the child that even the wind spoke a new language.

The woman and the man also took a long journey to that same city.
They met their child one night in July.

In the middle of all the new faces and the noise and the language they did not know,
there she was – their daughter – the baby girl in the little photo.

赵家楼饭店

浴池

早点春

新春旅

2013年 7 月 27 日

She wore a pale pink dress, with a
beautiful flower on it.

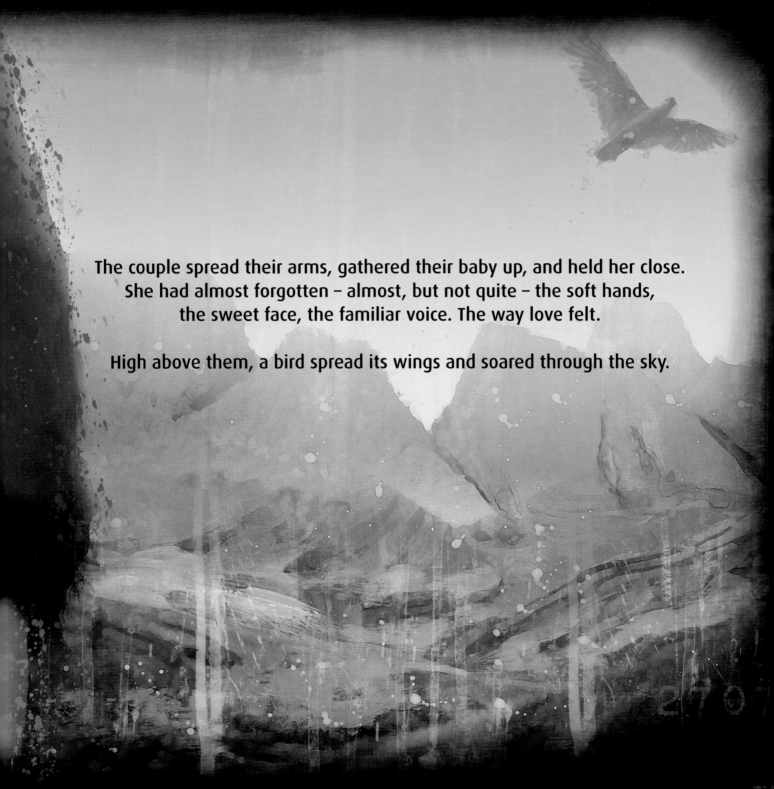

The couple spread their arms, gathered their baby up, and held her close.
She had almost forgotten – almost, but not quite – the soft hands,
the sweet face, the familiar voice. The way love felt.

High above them, a bird spread its wings and soared through the sky.

Then, one evening, the mother, the father, and their daughter flew – higher than the birds, higher than the clouds – away from the city and the land where the baby's roots had begun to grow.

Ahead, the sun rose, and with it shone the promise of new and wondrous things.

Years have passed.

Some days, the child hears a distant echo. She thinks of rice paddies,
of lotus flowers in the wind, of a little house with a pointed roof.
Sometimes, just before she sleeps, she whispers to the moon
that she is happy.

In their girl's wise eyes, her mother and father see the past joined with the present,

like a bridge that connects one place to another.

Just like the roots in a garden
weave together to become one plant,
the mother, father, and little girl
are bound to one another.
Their love joins them and reaches
to the other side of the earth.

On certain evenings, they sit, perfectly content,
and listen as night birds call out one last time
before settling into their nests.

And they thank a distant echo that travels on the night breeze
for allowing them to become a family.